Other titles in the DARK ENCHANTMENT series

Valley of Wolves

THERESA RADCLIFFE

PUFFIN BOOKS

PUFFIN BOOKS

Published by the Penguin Group
Penguin Books Ltd, 27 Wrights Lane, London w8 5TZ, England
Penguin Books USA Inc., 375 Hudson Street, New York, New York 10014, USA
Penguin Books Australia Ltd, Ringwood, Victoria, Australia
Penguin Books Canada Ltd, 10 Alcorn Avenue, Toronto, Ontario, Canada M4V 3B2
Penguin Books (NZ) Ltd, 182–190 Wairau Road, Auckland 10, New Zealand

Penguin Books Ltd, Registered Offices: Harmondsworth, Middlesex, England

First published 1996
1 3 5 7 9 10 8 6 4 2

Set in 13/15 pt Monotype Sabon
Typeset by Datix International Ltd, Bungay, Suffolk
Printed in England by Clays Ltd, St Ives plc

Chapter 1

THE TRAVELLER URGED his horse on. He was beginning to wish he'd not left the journey so late, or rather that he hadn't made it at all. The evening was closing in with alarming speed. The heavy clouds and biting wind could mean only one thing – snow was coming. The road through the mountains was flanked on either side by dark forests of fir and spruce. Even in daylight it was a sombre, forbidding place. Now, as dusk descended, it was the last place on earth the young lawyer wanted to find himself.

He was heading for the monastery of St Cleux, which lay on a remote hillside beyond the mountains. It was not so much the abbot's urgent summons that had brought him out, but the anticipation of a handsome fee. Mysteriously untouched by the plague, this isolated monastery had prospered in recent years and could still pay well for his services. Elsewhere plague, famine and harsh winters had devastated the country, bringing poverty and starvation to many. Wolves had left the mountains and forests and come down to the valleys to ravage towns and villages, carrying off unguarded livestock and unwary children or travellers.

The lawyer came upon the carriage quite suddenly, as the road turned a bend. It lay on its side, half off the road. Only a cluster of pine trees had prevented it slipping down the steep ravine. Pulling his horse to an abrupt halt, the shocked traveller kept his seat. He was uncertain whether he'd come upon the scene of some real misfortune, or whether this was an ambush set by evil brigands. He brought his horse forward cautiously, keeping alert to any sounds or movements that might indicate a hidden assailant. But as he drew nearer, he saw the gilded lilies and ravens on the carriage door and recognized at once the crest of the de Guise family. This was undoubtedly the carriage of the Count himself. Some terrible accident must have overtaken the Count and Countess de Guise.

The wind had dropped and flakes of snow were beginning to fall. The forest was strangely silent. The only sounds the traveller could hear were his horse's laboured breathing and his own heart pounding. He gripped the reins tightly. He desperately wanted to ride on, but knew he could not. He dismounted slowly, steeling himself against what he might find, trying to suppress the inexplicable anxiety that filled him. After all, the horses had gone, and this was surely a good sign. The unfortunate occupants, unable to right the carriage, would have surely ridden off to find help rather than spend a night on this dangerous, desolate highway.

The young lawyer could see nothing from the road side of the carriage. He moved slowly round, holding on to the chassis and wheels to prevent himself slipping down the bank. The Count, he knew it was the Count by his fine boots and clothing, was lying face down some way from the carriage. A servant was stretched out in a pool of blood close by. The Countess, wrapped in furs and fine ermine, lay half in, half out of the carriage door, the wound on her neck like a ribbon of garnet against the white fur.

The lawyer stood very still, as though needing time to take in the terrible scene in front of him. Then came the first howl, long, slow and mournful, jerking him back into action, to thoughts of his own safety. Then another and another, a rising chorus echoing through the forest. Wolves! He stumbled back up the bank. His horse was already moving its head and pawing the ground in alarm. He knew he had to reach his horse before fresh howling broke out and the terrified animal took off without him.

He approached the horse slowly, whispering soothing words. He mounted. He wanted to fly, to tear down the mountain, away from this awful scene, away from the wolves. But the snow was falling steadily now and it was nearly dark. One stumble, one slip and he could be thrown. Keeping a tight rein, he set off at a careful, steady pace.

As they moved slowly down the mountain, it seemed that the forest had come alive. Shadows were sliding between the trees. He could see the glimmer, the glint of flashing eyes and lean, hungry shapes stealing through the pines, padding silently towards the carriage. Suddenly he could bear it no longer. Grasping the horse's neck and digging in his heels, the lawyer set off at full gallop down the mountainside.

Somehow, by luck and good fortune, the young lawyer did reach the monastery of St Cleux that night and still in one piece. The surprised monks took him in out of the blizzard which was now raging. The trembling and frozen traveller told them his tale.

Nothing could be done that night, but the following morning the monks and the young lawyer set out through the snow to try and recover the unfortunate Count and Countess. They were joined on the road by a search-party from a town in the next valley, where the Count and his family had been expected the previous day. It seemed that the Count de Guise had been accompanied not only by his wife, but also his young son and heir, Jean-Pierre. The boy was some ten or eleven years old. Hearing this, the lawyer was thrown into great turmoil, for he had seen no sign of any child. But then nor had he, for sudden fear of the wolves, made any search of the area. He had not even looked inside the carriage itself. Suppose the boy was trapped in there. Would he have survived the night? What would they find?

At last they reached the scene. The forest was glistening now, white and shimmering in the cold sun. Snow covered the ground, the carriage, the overhanging trees; white snow, pure and unblemished. But beyond the road the trammelled snow – red now and horribly disturbed – revealed that the wolves had been at work. Only a few bloodied rags remained. No trace was ever found of the boy. It seemed that the whole noble family of de Guise had been wiped out in a single night.

CHAPTER II

MARIE STOOD SHIVERING by the window. The water in the well had been frozen. Her fingers were numb and cold. She tried to warm them with her breath. The sky was grey and the first flakes of snow were falling. She watched as they tried to settle on the cobbled yard, dissolving at first, but finally building up to a thin white layer. She hated this time of year and the memories it brought. It was now five years since the mysterious death of the Count and Countess, and of Jean-Pierre and her own father.

Her father had been with them on that fateful journey through the mountains. A favourite and well-loved servant, he had been head gardener to the estate. The magnificent rose garden and dovecot he had established were famous for miles around. Marie and her father had lived in a small cottage in the grounds of the château, protected from hardship and poverty. Her own mother was dead, but the Countess had shown great kindness to the little girl. Marie's earliest memories were of playing in the rose garden while her father worked. She and little Jean-Pierre tumbling among the fallen petals, chasing the pouting doves, walking hand in hand behind the Countess as she pointed out each rose to the children, telling them its history.

At first she had tried not to think back to those times, it had been too painful, but now those memories were her only comfort. Each day was endless drudgery, enough food but little else. Day after day, in return for a roof over her head, working for this strange and sullen master. Marie stared out over the estate, the snow disguising for a time the neglected wilderness. She could almost see the neat orchards and gardens as they had once been; the ordered fields and sheep-pens stretching out towards the hillside, the ornamental ponds and walkways. Gaston de Guise, a distant relative of the old Count, had dismissed all the estate workers and servants as soon as he'd arrived. The new Count had kept on only the orphaned girl who had no other home, as at twelve she was old enough to light a fire and see to his simple needs.

As Marie's glance returned to the courtyard, she noticed something white and fluttering by the broken fountain. A flutter, a slight movement and then quiet. Clutching her shawl, she ran out into the freezing yard. The bird lay motionless with its eyes closed, pitifully thin but still warm. It was a dove, no doubt a descendant of those she and Jean-Pierre had once cared for. She carried the bird inside, praying that it was still alive. She knelt down by the fire, cradling the dove in her hands. This little bird seemed suddenly to be a link with all she had loved and lost. Somehow it gave her new hope. She would save it, she wouldn't let it die.

Startled by a movement in the doorway, she looked up. Gaston de Guise was standing watching her. She clutched the bird to her. What was it about him that frightened her, and had so from the very first day? Was it the dark clothes draped like loose skin about his thin, hunched body? Was it the slender, waxen fingers, the long, tapering nails? Or was it the lingering smile that hung like a scar over his thin, grey lips? Lips that hardly moved, only the occasional snarl or sneer revealing the sharp, yellow points beneath.

It was impossible to tell the age of Gaston de Guise. His hair, though streaked with silver, was long, black and luxurious, falling to his shoulders. Thick, black, thundering brows met across his forehead, but the rest of his face was hairless. His white skin was smooth and flawless, almost transparent, delicate as the membrane across a sleeping snail. His eyes shone amber in the firelight, glinting like the ring he always wore.

The bird was moving in Marie's hands now, struggling weakly to be released. It hopped from her lap on to the floor, but collapsed at once, not strong enough to stand alone. Marie watched it fearfully, wondering what Gaston would do. She shuddered, imagining for a second the helpless bird held between those slender fingers, the neck snapped and broken, the gleam in his eye . . .

Marie could never tell what the Count

was thinking, or how he would be from one day to the next. Most hours of the day and some nights he spent in the cellars of the château. Sometimes he would emerge wild and elated, other times he'd be savage and remote. What he did down there she never knew. She had seen the packing-cases when he'd first arrived, the leather-bound books and manuscripts, tables and benches, glass jars, vessels and containers of every shape and size. But now the cellar doors were kept locked.

She had learned her duties, all he needed of her, very quickly, but she had never grown used to his strange ways. He was a man of extraordinary contradictions. He was fastidious about his wardrobe – the dark velvet suits and fine collars had to be brushed and hung each day – yet in his chamber he refused fresh linen. A couch of mangy hides and mottled fur served as his bed. He took his meals in the great hall on a tray of the finest silver. While she was still in the room, he picked over the food with the greatest refinement; the rabbit stews, the roast pheasants and other birds of his choosing. Yet when she returned, she would find the plates licked clean and laid out on the floor, the white bones chewed and sucked dry of every morsel.

Marie stretched out her hands to pick up the bird again. She didn't want the Count anywhere near it. She stroked it anxiously.

Gaston smiled slowly, 'What have we here, a pretty pigeon for the pot?'

Marie gasped.

Gaston laughed, his lip slightly curled. 'Keep the bird if it amuses you. But hurry with my meal. We have visitors this afternoon. Light the fire in the great hall.'

When he had gone, Marie laid the bird in a basket, placing by its side a few moistened crumbs. Then she quickly turned her attention to the rabbits boiling over the fire. She wondered who could be coming to the château – visitors were unheard of these days.

CHAPTER III

THE TWO MEN rode in silence towards the château. Theirs was a difficult and delicate mission, and they were unsure what kind of reception they would receive. The magistrate had met the new Count only once before, soon after his arrival. Although impressed by his great knowledge and learning, the man's strange aloofness had left an uncomfortable feeling. He was not the kind of man whose company you readily sought.

He had learned that Gaston de Guise had been drawn to the district, not only because of his unexpected inheritance, but by the nature of his scientific pursuits. These had already taken him to many other parts of the country. This remote, mountainous area now seemed the perfect place for him to complete his investigations into the nature of lycanthropy, that terrible phenomenon whereby a person is believed to assume the shape of a wolf. In recent years the district had witnessed some of the worst cases of lycanthropy in the country. Fortunately the magistrate had only had to deal with one case himself. The man had been convicted and burnt at the stake.

The second visitor, the doctor from the neighbouring town, had never met Gaston de Guise. He had attended the previous Count's family for many years. He now rode through the neglected estate with some dismay, wondering how a supposedly educated, sophisticated man could possibly tolerate such decay and wilderness.

Marie opened the door to the visitors.

'Presumably this girl would have known the boy,' the magistrate whispered to the doctor, who nodded in agreement. 'Good, then she may strengthen our case.'

Marie showed the men into the great hall where Gaston de Guise was waiting. Although initially put out by the impending interruption, he had decided that such dignitaries must surely be coming to contribute some important material to his research. He welcomed them warmly, dismissing Marie.

'Perhaps the girl could stay?' suggested the magistrate.

Gaston nodded. 'Now, how can I help you gentlemen. Have you brought me some new cases to study?'

The magistrate shook his head. 'We have come on a quite different matter, sir. You will recall the unfortunate accident five years ago in which your relatives the previous Count and his wife and son perished?' He nodded towards Marie, 'also this poor girl's father. Due to the circumstances,' he cleared his throat, 'no formal identification of the remains could be made. The boy was presumed lost with his parents, but many aspects of the case were never fully explained. The disappearance of the coachman and horses for instance.'

Gaston de Guise sat very still. His features would have betrayed nothing to even the most skilful observer. A polite, calm smile lingered on his lips, but his mind was racing. The coachman? Had he not been paid well enough? Had the man betrayed him?

The magistrate continued. 'A few months ago the abbot of St Cleux summoned your village priest. He had an extraordinary tale to tell. It seems that while a young monk was making his way to the monastery through the mountains, he came upon a ruined church in one of the remotest villages. Inside he found a poor creature. A creature, you could hardly call it a man or boy, such as he'd never seen before. It had long hair to its waist and was almost naked, despite the cold. Its nails were long and grimy; it seemed more animal than human. The monk was only sure the creature was human when it lifted its face and he saw a tiny glimmer of hope in its terrified, staring eyes. At first when he stretched out his hand, the thing flinched away. After much coaxing to show he meant no harm, he was sure he heard the hoarse, whispered words, "Help me." With some difficulty the young monk lifted him on to his horse and brought him to the monastery.

'For some weeks the monks looked after the boy, for clearly once shaved and bathed, the creature, though starved and piteously thin, appeared to be a boy of some fourteen or fifteen years. Terrible wounds to his wrists and ankles showed that he had been tethered in some way and his feet were torn and bleeding. Although over the weeks the wounds healed and he began to recover his health, the boy never spoke again. He would nod or shake his head in response to the monks' questions and was clearly intelligent.

'The boy's quiet and dignified manner impressed the abbot. Sometimes they would find him in the monastery library and he liked to walk in the gardens, studying the herbs and flowers. He seemed to know all the chants and responses in church, silently mouthing the words. This was clearly no lost or abandoned peasant child. The idea gradually grew in the abbot's mind that perhaps, the age being about right, that this was none other than the child of Count de Guise. Somehow the young boy Jean-Pierre had not perished with his parents at all.'

Marie was staring at the magistrate in disbelief and was trembling.

'Jean-Pierre, you say the boy is Jean-Pierre?'

Gaston de Guise showed no emotion whatsoever.

'I have not seen the boy myself,' said the

magistrate, 'and never knew him, but the doctor here has met him.'

The doctor nodded. 'Five years is a long time, but I am certain this boy is one and the same. Although he says nothing, I have detected some emotion when his name is spoken. No doubt there will be servants here who knew the child better than I.'

Gaston's mind was working fast. He had to know if he was in any way implicated in the death of the Count and Countess. The coachman had been the only weak link in his plan. The Count's fortune and these remote estates had been an answer to his prayers. A life's work devoted to a single cause, the secret so nearly unravelled. Driven from Paris by the authorities who had become suspicious of his experiments, he had at last found the place and the means to continue his work without disturbance. Nothing was going to stop him now. If the boy had survived, he would find a way to deal with him. But for now, pretence and great cunning was needed.

'The coachman, you still have no knowledge of the coachman who might shed some light on the matter?'

The magistrate shook his head. 'We know nothing of him.'

'And the boy,' continued Gaston, 'you say he cannot speak? You have not been able to discover what happened to him, to Jean-Pierre, if indeed it is him? You do not know how he has passed the intervening years?'

The magistrate shook his head.

'Yet you are certain that it is him?'

'We feel, sir, that all the evidence points that way. If it is the case, you will be aware that when the boy comes of age and if he is of sound mind, he will be the rightful Count de Guise, heir to these estates.'

Gaston smiled. 'Indeed, I shall have lost a title, but I will perhaps have gained a son.'

The magistrate bowed, impressed by his graciousness. 'The legal position will have to be clarified, but I would suggest that you remain here as his legal guardian for the present.'

'Of course, but first it must be established that the boy is who you claim.'

'You wish to pursue the matter in court?'

'I only want to be satisfied. Let the boy be brought here. Let us see whether the château awakens memories in him. And Marie, perhaps Marie will know him.'

Marie spoke very quietly. Her heart was pounding, her mind reeling. Jean-Pierre still alive, was it possible?

'I believe I will know him.'

'He is at present in my care,' said the doctor. 'I will bring him tomorrow.'

CHAPTER IV

GASTON DE GUISE could not sleep that night. He had to think, make plans. He was not going to let this disturbance, this small set-back, interfere with his work. They were nothing, these people, nuisances to be brushed aside. He would find a way to rid himself of this returned 'heir' in due course, a way that would not bring suspicion on himself. He must for the present show care and concern for the boy.

He was so nearly there; the secret, the power were in his grasp – to rearrange the very laws of nature, to transform matter. This knowledge was his. Nothing could stop him now. The true werewolf was not a product of witchcraft or the devil, it was a creation of science. After years of painstaking inquiry and experiment, he had learned the secret of the salve, the so-called 'magic' ointment that the peasants talked about. It was not magic at all. It was a precise union and combination of natural properties that brought about the transformation of the human form. In the hands of ignorant peasants, this ointment had produced monstrosities. Not only was the body changed, but the mind and soul as well, leading always to the werewolf's own destruction.

Yet he, Gaston de Guise, had discovered the ultimate secret – he had learned how to become the wolf and yet remain human. He could control the wolf's nature and use it to his own ends. Its power, its stealth, its cunning he could assume, while still retaining his own intellect and reason.

The application of the salve was a precise affair. The balance between the wolf's body and the human mind could only be maintained by the most accurate and careful measurements, and in this area his experiments were not complete. But once perfected, he knew the world lay before him. He threw off the wolf furs and began to make his way slowly, silently towards the cellars.

Marie lay on her small pallet by the kitchen fire. All night she tossed and turned, moving in and out of troubled dreams. Dreams filled with blue skies and fallen petals, the smell of summer and happy voices, her own and Jean-Pierre's. The white dove was there, the one she had found, now fully strong again and feeding from their hands. But then the snow would come, the sound of howling, grey shadows leaping through the tangled briars, red drops of blood . . . and she would wake screaming, crying out Jean-Pierre's name and her father's.

She sat up, wide awake now and listening. A long, low howl rang through the night. She'd heard the sound before, but never so close – it seemed to be coming from inside the château. She must be mistaken. She knew that the wolves would be moving nearer now. Each winter they left the mountains, moving through the woods and down the hillsides, coming to the valley in search of food.

The white bird was in the basket beside her. It was sleeping now, its head tucked into its breast. She stroked it gently, feeling the soft feathers. It was warm and alive. 'Let it be him. Let it be him tomorrow,' she said over and over to herself. 'Let it be Jean-Pierre.' The presence of the bird seemed to comfort her and she drifted at last into a calmer sleep.

All morning Marie watched for the carriage. She found it impossible to settle to anything. The bird seemed much stronger and offered some distraction. It fed from her hand now and took water from the dish she gave it. It hopped after her as she wandered anxiously from window to window.

The carriage arrived at last. Marie ran out into the courtyard. Gaston de Guise stepped forward to greet the doctor.

'How is the boy?' Gaston asked. 'Does he know where he is?'

'He says nothing,' said the doctor.

The doctor called to Marie. 'You must help me with him. He doesn't seem to want to leave the carriage.'

Marie moved slowly forward. Was it a cruel mistake – would she find a stranger there? If it was Jean-Pierre, would she really know him?

She looked into the carriage. He was sitting hunched in one corner, a dark cloak around his thin shoulders, his fair hair cut in a crude fashion across his brow, his hands folded. Marie knelt down in front of him.

'Jean-Pierre?' she whispered. He was older, taller and thinner, but as his eyes met hers, she knew.

'Jean-Pierre, it's me, it's Marie.'

He said nothing, but she saw that his eyes were filled with tears.

'You've come home,' she said gently. She took his hand and led him like a lost child out of the carriage and towards the château.

CHAPTER V

MARIE LED JEAN-PIERRE to the room she had prepared. A warm fire blazed in the grate. The doctor patted his hand.

'You're home, Jean-Pierre. You'll be well looked after here. I'll come and visit you soon.'

The boy was shaking and he didn't respond to the hand the doctor held out to him. The doctor turned to Marie. 'He needs good food and sleep. He'll mend in time.'

'What has happened to him?' whispered Marie. 'Why can't he speak?'

'Don't question him too much. He'll talk when he's ready.'

Marie stared at Jean-Pierre again remembering how they had once played and laughed together. His eyes seemed so vacant. She could not bear to see him like this.

'Jean-Pierre,' she whispered, 'it's me, Marie.'

He didn't respond, but she had seen that faint glimmer of recognition in the coach. That was all she could hang on to now. He would get well again, she was certain of that.

The doctor left the château, telling Gaston that he would return each week to check on the boy's progress.

Gaston bowed. 'What real chance is there that the poor boy will ever recover? In Paris such tragic cases are usually sent to the asylum, where there is little hope of a cure. Of course, as his legal guardian, I want everything possible to be done for him.'

The doctor shrugged. 'We can only wait. We'll speak again on my return.'

To Gaston's relief, however, the doctor was unable to fulfil his intentions, and for several weeks there were no further intrusions from the outside world. Winter set in and the high winds and drifting snow meant that the road to the château was impassable. Gaston was able to return to his work without further disturbance.

The boy's presence in the château hardly bothered him. Seeing Jean-Pierre slumped there in the chair, shivering and trembling, with that same blank expression on his face, he was sure the boy would never recover to claim his inheritance. When he'd stretched out his hand to touch him, the boy had shrunk back like a frightened dumb animal. This boy was no real threat to him. Gaston's own claim on the château was secure.

During the weeks that followed, Jean-Pierre was left in the sole care of Marie. Gaston did not come near the boy again. He knew nothing of the tiny changes that Marie noticed in Jean-Pierre each day.

Snow covered the château and the valley, cocooning them in a strange, silent world. It held them close. For hours she would sit in Jean-Pierre's room, staring with him out of the window at the whiteness, not knowing what was going through his mind. Sometimes when she could bear the silence no longer, she would begin to talk. She spoke about their past lives, their shared memories or about the little dove that now hopped and fluttered around his room.

Jean-Pierre still did not speak, but Marie noticed the small changes in him.

His eyes began to follow her as she moved about the room. She saw him watching the movements of the dove as it pecked at the crumbs she held for it, or as it hopped over to its dish of water.

Gradually Jean-Pierre seemed to do more and more for himself. She would find the cover pulled back over his bed, a chair put out for her, ready and waiting by the window. His tray would be left outside the door, the fire raked over. Slowly, very slowly he seemed to be coming alive. She would catch the glimmer of a smile as she entered the room, and his head turned to greet her. Once he stretched out his hand to touch the little bird, and one time, when she'd fled from Gaston, he put out his hand to wipe away the tears from her cheeks.

He ate well and grew stronger every day. There was plenty of food for them both during those weeks, as Gaston seemed to eat less and less of the meals Marie prepared. What little meat he ate, he took from the kitchen himself, tearing it still half-raw from the spit. Apart from these daily visits to the kitchen, Gaston kept more and more to the cellars.

Day and night his work now seemed to occupy him. Marie found that he had even dragged the furs and bedding from his chamber to these lower rooms where she was forbidden to go. Her fear and distrust of Gaston grew. Once so careful about his appearance, there now often seemed to be faint traces of blood and fur about his clothes and a dank smell hung from him. When he entered the room, the little dove always fluttered petrified against the pane, desperate to get out.

All Marie's time was spent caring for Jean-Pierre. He slept a great deal, his head resting peacefully on the pillow, his features calm, except on those nights when the howling came. Marie would go into his room and find him white and shaking, eyes staring round wildly. She would try to chatter gaily, reassuring him.

'Remember how excited we would be each year when we heard the first wolf. It meant the snow was coming and the ponds would soon be frozen over, ready to skate on. Every winter the wolves would leave the mountains and come down to the valley. We would watch the villagers hurrying to bring in their flocks of sheep and to round up their squealing pigs. For the hungry wolves would snatch any stray animal they could find. But they brought no real harm to us or the villagers.'

And yet in her heart Marie knew that this time it was different. The howls were not the usual cries of wolves, calling to each other as they roamed the valley slopes. These howls were different, not coming from a chorus of wolves, but were the cry of a solitary wolf – a savage, desperate, lonely howl unanswered by another beast. The howling always seemed so loud, so impossibly near that until she saw the look on Jean-Pierre's face, she wondered if she hadn't imagined it. After such occasions Jean-Pierre would sink back into himself and the look of pain and fear would return.

Marie dreaded those nights. She would wake with a start at the first howl, listening for Jean-Pierre. She would run to his room, sometimes finding him crying out in fear, as though wrestling with some phantom in his sleep. At other times she would hear him running backwards and forwards in his room and she would try to lead him gently back to bed. Once she had found him so wild and desperate, she could neither restrain nor wake him. He'd rushed barefoot from his room, out into the snow and moonlight. She'd followed him, calling his name. But he'd seemed neither to see nor hear her and had run towards the forest. She'd heard him calling his mother's name, '*Maman, Maman, no . . .*' His cries had cut through her, but she could do nothing to help him. At last he'd collapsed whimpering on the ground, trying to bury his head in the snow and block out the wolf's howling. She had led him back, still sleeping, to the château.

Jean-Pierre, however, continued to improve. One day when Marie brought books for him from the library, he touched her hand and she saw the words 'Thank you' forming on his lips. And then, louder, 'Thank you, Marie.'

CHAPTER VI

EACH DAY JEAN-PIERRE spoke a little more, but Marie mentioned nothing to Gaston. Just as with the bird, her instincts told her that at all costs, she must somehow protect Jean-Pierre from him. His slow recovery would be their secret until he was strong again. Until then she wanted to keep Gaston from him.

One afternoon as they sat by the window, the sun broke through the grey blanket of clouds, the first time for many days.

'The thaw is coming,' said Marie. 'The doctor will be visiting us again. You remember him?'

Jean-Pierre nodded, but he was thinking of other things. 'The garden, the rose garden, is it still there?'

'Yes, but it's very wild now.'

'We'll go there in the spring,' said Jean-Pierre.

They sat in silence for a moment, then Jean-Pierre looked up.

'I want to see her, Marie.'

Marie was startled and anxious. What could he mean?

'My mother, the picture. I want to see the picture.'

Of course, the portrait in the gallery. She nodded. 'I'll take you now.'

Jean-Pierre hesitated for a moment in the doorway. It was the first time he'd consciously left his room. 'He won't be there, will he?'

Marie shook her head – she knew Jean-Pierre was talking of Gaston.

'No, he'll be in the cellars. All of his time is spent there.'

Jean-Pierre followed Marie down the long, silent corridors. At each turn, he half expected his father's hounds to come tearing down the passages to greet him. But they saw and heard nothing as they made their way to the far side of the château.

The gallery was a magnificent, imposing room. Tall windows stretched the full length of one side, looking out on to the formal gardens. Pictures and fine tapestries hung on the other walls. A beautiful,

full-size portrait of the Countess domi-
nated the room. She was standing in the
rose garden. Dark, damask roses hung
around her white gown. Doves fluttered
above her head and petals lay strewn at
her feet. At her side stood two small children – Jean-Pierre and little Marie. Marie
remembered the dress she'd worn; the
Countess had had it specially made as her
own father could not have afforded the
rich silk.

Jean-Pierre and Marie now stood side
by side, looking up silently at the picture,
each lost in their own thoughts. Neither
heard the soft pad of Gaston's steps as he
drew near them.

'I see the patient is a little better today,'
Gaston spat the words, lips curled into a
snarl.

Marie and Jean-Pierre spun round.

Gaston stared angrily at Marie, 'Why
have you brought him from his room? I
gave you no such instruction.'

Jean-Pierre spoke slowly and softly.

'I am well, sir. I asked Marie to bring
me here.'

Gaston gave a shocked gasp, his face
drained. He was completely unprepared

for the change in Jean-Pierre. Recovering himself, he spoke with a faint smile, staring at Marie. 'You did not tell me that there had been such an improvement, indeed, any improvement.'

Marie faltered, 'We wanted to surprise you.'

Jean-Pierre moved forward, holding out his hand to Gaston.

'Marie tells me that you are my legal guardian, sir.'

Gaston bowed. 'Indeed, I am your only living relative. The good men who rescued you placed you in my care. The doctor will be very pleased at your progress. We will talk again when you are stronger.'

Gaston turned again to Marie. 'Take Jean-Pierre back to his room; he must rest.'

Jean-Pierre and Marie moved away uneasily. Gaston watched them go, fury seething inside him. The boy had recovered his senses. They had tricked him, deceived him. He would have to get rid of him after all. He was not going to lose the château now. He had found the ideal setting for his work, and at last his experiments had been successful. He'd achieved his dream. He could now begin to explore the boundaries of all living experience. He would learn to assume the form of any beast or bird. Nothing was going to stop him. He would use his new knowledge and power to destroy the boy.

That night, exhausted by the day's events, both Marie and Jean-Pierre fell into a deep sleep. Their dreams were not disturbed by the long, low howls echoing from the depths of the château. They slept on, unaware of the soft pad of paws moving upwards and along the winding corridors; the steady pant of the beast as it made its way through the château; the snarl of delight as it slipped out into the moonlight.

Gaston paused on the steps, feeling the cold air rushing through his fur, his excitement rising. He turned his head towards the château, thinking of Jean-Pierre and Marie. A quick pounce, a snap of the neck, it would be over quickly. He had perfected his hunting skills in the forest – no creature could avoid him once his mind was set. He was stronger and fiercer than any wolf. The wolves themselves had soon slunk away, leaving the forest to him. Only one wolf, the pack leader, had dared to challenge him. Their fight had been swift and furious. The wolf's skin now lay on his chamber floor. He leapt from the steps and ran silently through the snow and biting wind towards the village.

CHAPTER VII

THE DOCTOR VISITED at last. He was surprised and pleased by the change in Jean-Pierre and recommended to Gaston that the boy be allowed to do whatever he wanted. He needed to resume as normal a life as possible. He congratulated Gaston and Marie on the care they had given Jean-Pierre and pronounced him well on the road to recovery.

'I would like,' said Jean-Pierre, 'to assist my guardian with the running of the estate.'

'In due course,' said Gaston. 'One step at a time, isn't that right, doctor?'

The doctor nodded. 'I will come back in a few weeks. Marie will see me to the door.'

When alone with Marie, the doctor questioned her further. 'Does Jean-Pierre speak of what happened during those years?'

Marie shook her head. 'He says nothing

of that time. But on those nights when the howling comes, I hear him screaming terribly in his sleep, and pacing his room . . .'

The doctor interrupted, 'You have heard it here then, the wolf?'

Marie nodded. 'All winter and so close the sound seems to echo through the walls. And sometimes even now, though the snows have gone and there should be no wolves in the valley.'

'You've heard nothing from the village?'

'You are the first person we have seen since the winter.'

'I didn't want to speak of it in front of Jean-Pierre, but you must take great care if you leave the château. A black shadow has fallen over the valley. Wolves we are used to dealing with; each year they come down from the mountains and one or two sheep or goats are taken from a broken pen. But this creature is different. Those who have glimpsed it say it is a huge beast of extraordinary cunning, as large as a man. Stable doors have been opened, the latches lifted, secure pens torn down. A watch has been set up and traps have been dug. People are beginning to fear for their lives. They say it is no ordinary wolf.

Indeed, it has driven all the other wolves away. They say it has been sent by the devil . . .'

Gaston stood unseen in the shadows, watching the doctor leave, a faint smile playing on his lips. 'Thank you, doctor,' he murmured, 'thank you for the news you have brought.'

He was prepared. No goose-traps or men with dogs would ever catch him. At every step he would outwit these peasants. Nothing could stop him now. He longed for night to come, the time when he could assume the wolf's shape. He longed to feel the cold air on his face, the dark skies above him, running fast and free in his restless hunt for prey. During the day the walls and confines of the château seemed like a prison, and his man's body a slow and clumsy thing compared to the strength and swiftness of the wolf.

That night Gaston prowled the silent corridors, thinking and planning. Destroying Jean-Pierre without bringing suspicion on himself was now his first concern. He paused for a moment outside the boy's room. Standing on his back legs, he slowly lifted the latch to the heavy door with his snout and pushed it open.

Jean-Pierre was sleeping deeply, the cover moving gently up and down with his breath. The neck of the boy's nightshirt lay open and his lips were slightly apart. Gaston moved closer. He wanted to sink his teeth into the white flesh . . . But no, this wasn't the right time, and yet . . .

A slight movement on the far side of the room caught his attention. The white dove had woken from its perch on the window-sill. It was flattening itself against the pane in a desperate attempt to escape. Gaston turned from the bed and leapt towards the window. He seized the bird in his jaws. In a short time just a few feathers remained. Gaston ran from the room.

That night the village suffered its worst losses. Two geese were taken, a barn broken into and a goat killed, and a woman was attacked in her own cottage.

CHAPTER VIII

SPRING HAD COME at last to the château. The briars and roses stretched out their long stems in new-tangled profusion. Jean-Pierre began work in the rose garden. He threw himself into the task of taming the wild thicket. Marie had been inconsolable after the strange disappearance of the little dove, and so Jean-Pierre was determined to restore the dovecot for her. She joined him whenever she could, pleased to be out of the château and away from Gaston.

Although Gaston usually spent his days in the cellars, that morning Marie had heard the heavy slamming of the oak door and so knew that Gaston had left the château early for some reason.

Jean-Pierre had been outside since early morning. Every daylight hour he spent in the garden, trying to restore some order to the wilderness. At midday Marie had joined him and they had eaten their meal together. When they had finished, they lay back on the damp grass, staring up at the blue sky and racing white clouds.

'I'm sure the doves will come back,' said Jean-Pierre, 'and the garden will be as it used to be.'

Marie almost allowed herself to share his hopes. After all, the nights had become more peaceful and Jean-Pierre was well again.

At last Marie reluctantly slipped away. There was work to be done in the kitchen.

Jean-Pierre continued working in the garden until early evening. He was clearing the path that led to a small summer-house in the centre of the garden. It was slow work as the roses had formed an impenetrable barrier. Suddenly he heard a sound. It was faint, still far away in the distance, but it was a sound he knew. It was the cry of hounds, of dogs closing in on their quarry. He stood motionless for a moment, unable to move, trying to push back the fear that rose in him and to push away the terrible memories that were flooding back. He was seeing it all again, remembering the sound, the awful sound growing in his head as the baying drew nearer and nearer.

His ankle was throbbing, raw and bleeding where he'd worked to cut the chain. So many weeks, months secretly filing it through, waiting for this moment when he'd be free. At night they'd kept him tied up with the dogs on a bed of straw. He was chained up just out of the dogs' reach and was left to share their food if he could be quick enough to seize it; the bones they threw down, the husks of bread.

During the long days the charcoal-burners took him with them to the forest to help chop the logs and stack their fires. If he didn't work, he wasn't fed. For months he'd been filing away at the chain with a small piece of stone. Now at last he was free. He crept away into the forest, slowly, silently at first, fearing to wake the sleeping dogs, then broke into a run down, down the mountain.

They found him gone at daybreak. They took the dogs and tracked him all that morning. He was running slower now, no strength left. He could hear the dogs, closer and closer now, the fearful baying as they drew in, the shouts of the men . . .

It was all coming back; it was happening all over again.

Jean-Pierre ran from the rose garden just as the group of villagers and their dogs reached the outer gate to the château. The dogs were straining hard on their leashes. The front runners pulled on towards the château steps, so only the dogs bringing up the rear caught sight of Jean-Pierre. Their masters did not see this new quarry. In the frenzy and excitement, two dogs broke free and tore towards him. The men swore at their dogs, calling them back. Jean-Pierre, cut off now from the château, could only turn back into the garden. Perhaps he could reach the summer-house.

Desperately he ran through the briars, trying to force a path; this shelter was his only hope. The dogs dashed after him, yelping and snarling. They plunged through the thorns and wild undergrowth in pursuit. Jean-Pierre's head and arms were now torn and bleeding, the brambles clutching his legs and feet. He forced himself on, deeper and deeper into the thicket. The men had entered the garden now; he heard their voices. He felt the dogs' hot breath on his legs and then there was blackness.

'Here, over here,' cried the men, 'the dogs have got something.'

'It's a boy. Call them off. It's the son of the last Count. Pull the dogs away.'

They laid Jean-Pierre on the grass and ran to the château for help. Marie came first, followed by Gaston, who ordered the doctor to be called.

The men gathered round, apologizing, 'The dogs brought us here, sir. The wolf's trail led us to the estate. We tried to pull them off . . .'

'The wolf?' asked Gaston. 'Has there been another attack?'

'A child from the village, attacked in broad daylight, playing in the orchard. Her father drove away the brute and called the watch. The dogs followed the trail . . .'

Jean-Pierre was carried inside. Tenderly Marie bathed his wounds. The dogs had not harmed him, but the roses and brambles had left deep gashes on his arms and legs.

The doctor arrived at last. Marie was beside herself as Jean-Pierre had still not moved. After all this, was she to lose him again?

Finally Jean-Pierre opened his eyes. The terror in them gradually faded as he realized he was safe. He clutched Marie's hand. 'Don't let them find me and take me back, not again.'

'It's all right, Jean-Pierre,' said the doctor. 'Nothing's going to happen to you here. These men and their dogs out there were just from the village.'

'They haven't got me. They won't get me again. I remember now, I ran away . . .'

'Rest now,' said the doctor. 'You can tell us later.'

Jean-Pierre stared up at Marie, 'You won't leave me?'

Marie smiled. 'I won't leave you.'

The doctor took Gaston aside. 'The boy's had a bad fright that is somehow connected with events in the past. Now I must get back to the child in the village. I don't think she'll survive the night. As I feared, there may be more to this wolf business. God forbid we have another werewolf in our midst.'

Gaston smiled as the doctor hurried away, pleased how successful his plan had been. The villagers had seen and followed the wolf as he'd intended. He'd managed to lure them and their dogs right to the château. He had planted the first seeds of suspicion.

CHAPTER IX

EARLY ONE MORNING the following week, Gaston crept out before sunrise. A white mist hung over the valley. He slipped like a grey shadow over the ground, heading for the meadows where the shepherd boys brought the sheep to graze.

He lay down behind a fallen willow tree and waited. He heard their whistles as they drove the sheep along the track and the distant bleating of a ewe that had become separated from the herd. The older boys came into view first. They marched along cheerfully giving orders to the younger lads, whose job it was to round up the stragglers. A small, blond-haired boy was shaking his head. 'Not again,' he wailed, 'I'm tired,' but he was still sent back to fetch the straying sheep. The rest of the group moved off towards the far end of the meadow.

The child saw a flash of grey fur, the

snapping jaws and that was all. One scream and he hit the ground. The older boys tore back over the meadow. Gaston stood over the boy for a moment and then raised himself up on hind-legs, snarling at the mob that rushed him. Stones, sticks, anything they could find the boys began to hurl at him. Gaston turned then and ran, slipping past them down the meadow. They followed him. Gaston felt the stones whistling past him. Some struck home and he cried out as the sharp edges pierced his fur. He could have easily outstripped them, but he had to keep in their sights, leading them to the very edge of the de Guise estate. Then he disappeared, returning to the cellars to lick his wounds.

In the village the talk was of nothing but this beast that stood on two legs and screamed like a man. At the château the days slipped by without further event. Jean-Pierre found that Gaston was spending a lot more time with him, and he began to look at his relative in a new light.

'He's strange I know,' Jean-Pierre told Marie, 'but he's a man of science, obsessed by his work. He seems quite happy for me to think about running the estate.

His work leaves him no time for such things. He has also agreed to take on some servants. I have explained your position in my family's household and that you should not be doing the kind of work he makes you do. I know he has made us all live frugally, but it seems he did not want to spend my father's fortune, which is still intact. But now we shall have a number of servants and you will be mistress of the house.'

Marie smiled, certain that Gaston would not keep his word, worried how child-like Jean-Pierre's visions were. She doubted very much that things would work out as he'd planned.

Marie herself saw no change in Gaston, except that in Jean-Pierre's presence he spoke more considerately to her. At other times he treated her like the lowliest of servants. Early one morning he appeared in the kitchen, Jean-Pierre having already begun work in the rose garden.

'Light the fire in the hall,' Gaston ordered. 'We have guests today; the magistrate and doctor are coming. There's no need to mention the visit to Jean-Pierre, do you understand? It's of no concern to him. Bring wine when they arrive.'

Marie watched the magistrate and doctor ride up to the château, just as they had done on that cold winter morning so many weeks before. She took them into the hall where Gaston was waiting. When she had brought the wine, Gaston dismissed her to the kitchens.

Marie left the men, quietly closing the oak door behind her, but she did not return to her work. Why had Gaston sent for them, and why didn't he want Jean-Pierre to know? The door-frame was old and warped, leaving a crack wide enough to see through. Marie pressed herself close to the frame and so could hear and see the men quite clearly.

Gaston was speaking. 'These are difficult and troubled times, gentlemen. As you know, the study of lycanthropy has been my life's work and I believe I can help you.'

The magistrate spoke first. 'We do not know that this is what we are dealing with. I have not completed my investigations.'

'No, indeed,' continued Gaston, 'but

what I have heard from the villagers and the doctor here has caused me great unease. I myself am now certain that some terrible evil has been unleashed among us. It is not unusual for wolves to take livestock from the valley in winter. But these attacks have continued well into the spring in broad daylight, even behind locked doors. The beast described is of a great size and has human characteristics as well. I am sure this creature is indeed a werewolf . . .'

The magistrate at this point seemed about to interrupt him, but Gaston held up his hand. '. . . And further,' Marie saw Gaston pass his hand over his face in a gesture of anguish and despair, 'further, gentlemen, and this is the most difficult part of the whole affair. I have come increasingly to believe – I wish I could remain silent, but my conscience will not allow it – I have come to believe that this werewolf is none other than my own relative, the boy who has become a son to me. I believe that Jean-Pierre is the werewolf.'

CHAPTER X

MARIE THOUGHT SHE was going to fall. Her head was spinning and she was shaking. She pressed herself against the wall, terrified she would betray herself. How could it be possible? It couldn't be true? She could see that the doctor had got up and was pacing up and down.

'What are you saying?' he gasped. 'This is madness. What you suggest is preposterous.'

Gaston shook his head. 'I wish it were, but don't you see? It's true he appears to have regained his senses, but I fear that this apparent recovery is an illusion. He has been terribly altered by what he has suffered, those years in the mountains . . .'

The magistrate interrupted, 'Has he spoken of those times?'

The doctor nodded, 'He has told Marie how he was found by a remote band of charcoal-burners. That he was kept chained like a dog among dogs and forced to work for them until he managed to escape to the place where the monk found him.'

Gaston continued, 'My researches have found that lycanthropy can take two forms. In the first case, and this is true lycanthropy, men and women, by the use of what they believe to be magical salves and ointments, are able to transform themselves into real wolves. The second form is feigned lycanthropy. In this instance the lycanthrope is merely someone mad and deranged who believes he is a wolf. He often disguises his body with a wolfskin and thus clothed begins to act like a wolf.

'Over these past weeks I have reluctantly come to believe that Jean-Pierre's experiences in the mountains and the gruesome death of his parents have twisted his mind so terribly that he is now compelled to re-enact the things he saw. He seeks to overcome his fear of the wolf by becoming one.'

The magistrate interrupted Gaston again, 'But what proof have you? This is all supposition . . .'

Gaston raised his arms. 'Do you think

that I make these accusations lightly? No, no, I tell you. I have lain awake at night praying that it is not so – but all the signs point to him.

'Ask yourselves, when did the first attacks begin? Was it not after Jean-Pierre's return? And after each attack has not the wolf been tracked coming towards this estate? At first I convinced myself that the wolf was taking this route back to the mountains. But, if so, why did the dogs not follow it further? Why did the trail always end here? And you yourself, doctor, were called to attend Jean-Pierre after the attack on the child in the orchard. The dogs had pursued their quarry right to the château garden. Who was found there trying to make his escape but Jean-Pierre himself?'

'No, no, it's not true,' Marie wanted to scream. She'd been with Jean-Pierre that day or at least part of the day, but then she'd left him working in the garden. Could he have slipped away, gone down to the village? Oh God, no, it wasn't possible.

The magistrate was talking now. 'Have you actually confronted the boy with any of this?'

Gaston shook his head. 'What point would there be? He would deny it all, even this . . .'

Gaston drew out something from a sack that he'd had under the table. It was a wolfskin, the top part of the head and upper jaw still intact like a terrible mask.

'Look here at these fastenings, the dried blood on the fur . . . and these too I have found in his room.' He emptied the sack on to the table. A dagger and a wooden claw studded with curved iron nails tumbled out. 'Instruments of evil.'

Marie could not believe it. There had been no dagger, no claw, no wolfskin hidden in Jean-Pierre's room. She would have known, wouldn't she? What awful nightmare was this starting over again? But the doctor and magistrate, they seemed to believe Gaston.

Gaston was still speaking. 'The boy cannot help himself – even within the château, in his own room, the girl's tame dove destroyed . . .'

The magistrate interrupted, 'If the boy is indeed responsible for the attacks, then he must be taken from here and secured, but we still need more proof. That burden will have to rest with you, Gaston. You are his guardian; he is in your charge. At night the château door must be locked and secured. You must know where he is at all times. If he leaves the estate, you must follow him. You will need to catch him in the act . . .'

Marie fled before the door was opened. Her mind was reeling. She stumbled down the stone steps into the kitchen, her eyes blinded by tears. How could Jean-Pierre possibly be capable of such a thing? Surely she would know if he was still ill or mad? But it seemed she no longer knew anything, the whole world was crumbling. Let it be Gaston who was mad and evil, not Jean-Pierre. Don't let it be Jean-Pierre, she prayed.

CHAPTER XI

FOR THE NEXT two weeks there were no more reports of wolf attacks and the people began to go about their daily lives again without fear. But Marie herself could not forget. She was frightened. And as hard as she tried, she could not quite get out of her mind the awful possibility that it might be Jean-Pierre, that, indeed, he might be ill because of the terrible things that had happened to him. She could not forget how she had seen him out in the snow on those nights when she had heard the wolf. These thoughts put a shadow between them, an uneasiness. She wanted to tell him, to warn him, but she couldn't bear to admit her own fears to him. She was uncertain of anything any more, except that she loved him.

'Don't let it be true,' she prayed, 'don't let it be true.'

Jean-Pierre noticed this strangeness and change in her.

'What is it, Marie? Have I done something?'

'I'm tired, that's all,' she would say. He'd begged her to see the doctor, but she'd refused. 'No, there's nothing the matter.'

It was Jean-Pierre who now felt strained and awkward. They had been so close, so happy. He knew that their childhood friendship had grown into something more. He could not imagine his life without her; he loved her. A few weeks before he had been almost sure that she felt the same as he did. He longed to take her in his arms and tell her how he felt. But now she seemed so distracted, so distant, perhaps he had been wrong. Perhaps she *was* just tired. Caring for him by herself all those weeks had been too much for her. Jean-Pierre began to ask Gaston daily when the new servants would arrive.

Gaston had told him, 'You can go to the village yourself tomorrow and arrange it with the old steward. You remember the way?'

Jean-Pierre nodded.

'Be careful of the goose-traps as you go

through the meadow. The steward's house is the first in the village.'

The next morning Jean-Pierre set off very early. He said nothing of his errand to Marie. As well as seeing the steward, he was intending to bring her some fresh eggs and butter. He remembered the wild irises that grew by the river and how they used to gather them together. He would stop on his way back to pick some for her.

Marie had seen Jean-Pierre slip out. She'd been down by the well drawing water. Trembling and anxious, she quickly put down her bucket and crept after him. Where could he be going? Why hadn't he told her? Where was Gaston? Was Gaston watching him too?

It was a beautiful day and the sun was already warm. A light breeze blew on Jean-Pierre's face, bringing the scent of clover from the fields. Once Marie was well again, once he was Count and running the estate, everything would be all right. He remembered every part of the path; the stile that led down to the river, the track that led to the hazel copse.

Jean-Pierre had just reached the last meadow when his thoughts were suddenly disturbed by a tremendous honking and squawking. It was the sound of a goose calling, obviously in some distress, and seemed to be coming from a large pit on one side of the track. This must be one of the goose-traps that Gaston had mentioned. Jean-Pierre stared down. A number of sharply pointed stakes were sticking upwards, ready to impale any wolf or other creature that might jump down to seize the unfortunate goose that was tethered at the bottom. The poor bird appeared half starved. Jean-Pierre took some bread from his pocket and tossed it down. The grateful creature stopped its noise at once. Kneeling down, Jean-Pierre peered over the edge of the pit to take a closer look.

Gaston was waiting for him with a heavy cudgel in his hand and a sack on his back. His lip curled; how simple it was, how easily Jean-Pierre fell into his plans. A snarl appeared on his lips . . .

At that moment Marie entered the meadow. She saw Jean-Pierre bending over the pit and then saw Gaston. Her mind reeled.

'Jean-Pierre!' she screamed.

Startled, Jean-Pierre spun round to find Gaston close behind him and Marie running screaming towards him.

'My boy,' exclaimed Gaston, stretching out his hand as though to help him up. 'I thought you were going to fall.'

Marie stared at Gaston, saying nothing. She glanced at the sack. The truth hit her. She was breathing fast. She had to stay calm, not give anything away, not let him suspect that she knew. He had been lying, it was all lies. He'd planted the lies so that he could destroy Jean-Pierre.

'Go back to the château, both of you,' said Gaston. 'It is too soon for Jean-Pierre to be out on his own. I will visit the steward myself.'

Jean-Pierre and Marie turned silently and left. Jean-Pierre couldn't understand what was going on, only sensing the tension between Gaston and Marie. The pleasure of the day had gone.

Gaston watched them walk away. He cursed Marie. What had she seen? What did she know? He would make sure she didn't spoil his plans again.

Jean-Pierre and Marie walked in silence. They could feel Gaston staring after them as they went. Only when they'd left the meadow did they take each other's hands and begin to run. They reached the rose garden at last and scurried into the summer-house. Marie sank on to the floor, trembling and shaking, trying to compose herself.

Jean-Pierre lifted her up. 'What is it, Marie? What's happened that's so terrible?'

She spoke at last, slowly, calmer now. 'He's trying to kill you, Jean-Pierre. He was about to push you into the pit. He had the sack with him, with the claw and the wolfskin.'

'What do you mean? What are you talking about?'

'He's made them believe that you're still ill, Jean-Pierre, that you're some kind of terrible monster. He claims that you're the werewolf – the wolf that's been terrorizing the village. He's made the doctor, and everybody, believe it.'

Jean-Pierre was white now, white with anger and rage. For a moment he said nothing.

'Jean-Pierre, I'm sorry. I'm sorry. I love you. I didn't know what to believe. Forgive me, Jean-Pierre. I love you so much. I couldn't tell you.'

Marie was crying now, but then Jean-Pierre was holding her and kissing her.

'I love you, Marie. You're the only thing that matters to me. Gaston can't touch me. Everything will be all right as long as we're together.'

Marie gently kissed him. Then they sat for a moment very quietly, each lost in their own thoughts. The early roses were in full bloom now. Their fragrance drifted down, overpowering in the warm sunshine. Many small birds had returned, their song filling the garden.

Marie felt a sudden shiver. The image of a long-forgotten dream returned. 'It was him, Jean-Pierre. Gaston killed the dove. He told them you'd done it. Oh God, I hate him and I'm frightened, frightened for you.'

'He won't try anything again, not yet. We must get to the magistrate, tell him everything. Gaston mustn't know that we suspect anything. We must try to carry on as if nothing has happened.'

Jean-Pierre held her. 'It's going to be all right, Marie. We'll fight him together.'

CHAPTER XII

THE FOLLOWING DAY Jean-Pierre spoke to Gaston. He had to find a way in which he and Marie might leave the château without raising Gaston's suspicions.

'When the new servants arrive,' explained Jean-Pierre, 'Marie will take on a different position in the household and she will need some fine new clothes. I would like to go with her to town to choose some.'

Gaston thought for a moment, then replied with a smile.

'Indeed, my boy, indeed Marie shall have some new clothes. She shall go this afternoon to buy all the cloth and ribbons she needs. But I'm afraid there are some accounts that will keep us both busy until this evening. She must go alone.'

Jean-Pierre was anxious about Marie making such a long journey on her own, but it was one Marie had made many times before with her father. She knew the path well. For most of the way it ran along the outskirts of the forest, only turning for a short distance into a much denser, darker part of the wood.

'I shall be all right,' she told Jean-Pierre. 'I've lived near these forests all my life. It's you who must take care.'

'But the werewolf . . . it still hasn't been caught.'

'There have been no attacks in the forest,' she reassured him.

Jean-Pierre handed her his father's hunting knife. 'Please take this with you. Go straight to the magistrate and tell him everything.'

'Don't worry, I shall be back before it's dark.'

Jean-Pierre kissed her gently on the cheek. 'Take care.'

'Come to the edge of the path and wave me goodbye.'

Marie set off down this path that led to the edge of the forest. It was later than she'd realized. She'd have to walk quickly if she was to cover the seven miles to town and back before dark. She stopped for a second and looked back. Jean-Pierre was still watching her. She felt her heart racing. He loved her.

Jean-Pierre was not the only person watching her. Gaston stood on the steps of the château. His lips twisted into a slight smile. How easily they fell into his hands. The girl was not going to spoil his plans again. He would get rid of them both at one stroke. They would find her the next day, savaged in the forest with Jean-Pierre the dead werewolf at her side.

Gaston was still on the steps when Jean-Pierre came in.

'I've been waiting for you, my boy. The estate's accounts are ready for you to examine. I can't join you straight away as I'd planned. I'm at a crucial stage with an experiment and the work can't be left. I shall join you in the library later.'

CHAPTER XIII

JEAN-PIERRE PACED the library angrily. There had been nothing of real importance to keep him there. As far as he could tell, all the accounts looked in order. He just had to sit and wait for Gaston.

The library was situated in the east wing, immediately above the chambers where Gaston spent so much of his time. Had Jean-Pierre been in his own room or in the hall or kitchens, he probably would not have heard the sound at all. It was muffled at first, like a sound that was being suppressed, controlled – but it was still a sound that made the hairs on his neck rise. He'd heard it before at night, in his dreams. Then it had been unrestrained. Now it was more tentative, but it was still a howl, a wolf's howl.

Jean-Pierre gripped the edge of the table. At night his senses had been confused. The sound had seemed near by, yet he knew it could only come from the forest. Now, however, there was no mistaking it. The sound was definitely coming from inside the château, from the rooms below him. He couldn't move. It was a fear he could not control; it swept over him, paralysing him.

What was Gaston playing at? What fearful experiments had induced him to bring a wild beast into the château? Had Gaston perhaps captured the beast that had been terrorizing the village? What was this secret work that kept Gaston so occupied?

Jean-Pierre left the library and began to make his way slowly down to the lower chambers. He descended a long, stone stairway. At last he reached a small window that had been cut into the wall just above the final flight of steps. From here Jean-Pierre could see down into the dim cellar.

He had expected to see some kind of cage where the wolf was secured and to see Gaston at work at his bench. He peered through the gloom. There was no sign of Gaston at all and no cage – instead all he saw was a huge creature, a wolf roaming free and unrestrained. Jean-Pierre shuddered. What was Gaston thinking of? How could he let such an animal loose?

The wolf was pacing up and down the floor. Its body was huge, its grey coat peppered silver and black. But its tail was missing, making the animal look curiously stunted and misshapen. From time to time it stopped pacing and sat in the middle of the floor with its head flung back. A long, low howl issued from its throat.

Jean-Pierre saw the pointed, set-back ears of the wolf, the high brow, the strong, yellow fangs. He saw the glowing amber eyes, slanting and piercing, yet curiously thoughtful. Jean-Pierre watched in horror as the creature then stood up on its hind legs. It looked from left to right, pausing for a moment, and then with its strong snout it began to lift the latch that fastened the door.

This creature was no ordinary wolf. Jean-Pierre realized the awful truth. The village rumours had been right. The beast that had stalked them was indeed a werewolf.

Jean-Pierre turned and fled back up the

steps. He slid between two pillars in the hallway, not daring to move or breath, terrified that the thing might see or smell him. But he had to see where the animal was going. His only thought now was for Marie, out there alone in the forest.

He heard the scratch of claws on stone as the thing bounded up the steps and into the hallway. It stood still for a moment, again turning its head left and right as though checking that it was unobserved. Then it leapt towards the heavy oak door. Jean-Pierre watched as the creature lifted the bar and slipped out into the daylight.

He crept forward. He dare not lose sight of it. The animal bounded down the steps and across the courtyard. It seemed to sniff the air and then smell the ground. It looked up again. Take the path to the village, prayed Jean-Pierre, or across the fields. But no, with a final sniff of the ground, it began to run towards the forest path, the one Marie had taken.

Jean-Pierre's heart was pounding. The creature was moving faster now with a steady, loping gait. Jean-Pierre began to run. How could he keep up with it? He mustn't lose sight of it. He had to reach Marie before the creature did.

He ran on and on, in a kind of daze. The trees flashed by him. It seemed that once again all he could hear was the terrible howling in his ears. He saw the wolves in the trees. He saw the carriage. He saw his mother and father. He was running and running, but not away this time. This time he would save them, this time he would kill the wolves.

CHAPTER XIV

MARIE WALKED BRISKLY along the path. The first part of the journey took her along the edge of the forest, where the trees were mostly birch and openly spaced. The sun shone down through their branches and flowers lined the little path that ran along the edge of a fast-flowing stream.

The path had begun to move away from the stream now, turning deeper into the forest. It was quieter here and darker. The dense, overhanging trees allowed little light through. She could hear her own soft tread on the pine needles, the jolt of the basket against her hip. She felt her heart beating faster. She would be glad when the path turned back towards the stream and the open glade beyond.

A sudden sound startled her, the cry of a large bird. She heard the clatter of branches as it soared away. Then silence again. She walked on, alert now, ears straining to every sound. There was the rustle of a leaf, the crack of a snapping twig. She spun round. Was something behind her, following her? She forced herself on, slowly at first, listening intently to her own steps. Then another sound, she was certain now, a steady pad, pad over the pine needles. She began to run, her hair catching on the lower branches of the trees, not daring to look back. The animal, whatever it was, was closing in on her, she was sure of that. She breathed deeply, trying to stop the panic, trying to think, trying to keep some distance.

Suddenly Marie stopped. She turned. Whatever it was, wolf or other wild beast, she couldn't outrun it, but nor would she let it pounce on her from behind. She took Jean-Pierre's knife from the basket and stood still on the path, gripping the weapon in both hands, waiting and listening. She stared at the bend in the path where she expected the thing to appear. She listened – nothing, no sound. Had it only been her own footsteps that she had heard? Where was it? Why didn't it come? She was ready.

The creature sprang from nowhere, a

grey shadow hurtling towards her. It had crept past her through the forest and doubled back. It pounced, claws bared, teeth glistening. As it knocked her to the ground, its claws tore her cloak and the knife flew from her hands. As Marie tried to reach the knife, the creature turned. Marie saw its face now, close to hers. She saw the cold, staring, amber eyes and in that instant knew who and what the creature was. It lunged towards her, reaching for her throat.

A scream rang in her ears, not from her. She heard her name. Jean-Pierre was racing towards her. He threw himself on the wolf's back, grasping its neck with his bare hands. With a desperate snarl the wolf leapt round, flinging him to the ground.

It was Jean-Pierre the creature came at now, claws outstretched, drooling fangs, jaws snapping. Marie was forgotten. She ran for the knife and seizing it in both hands, she turned and struck. She took off one of the wolf's paws with a single stroke. The creature howled and backed away, screaming in pain, its eyes dim with fury and hatred. Then it turned away into the depths of the forest.

Jean-Pierre and Marie stood very still, both shaking terribly.

'I thought I was going to lose you too.' Tears were streaming down Jean-Pierre's face.

Marie pointed in the direction the wolf had taken. 'That creature, it wasn't an ordinary wolf.'

'I know,' said Jean-Pierre, 'it came from the château. I followed it here. Gaston had been keeping it . . .'

Marie was no longer listening. She was looking at the ground, staring intently at the severed paw. She shuddered, gripping his hand tightly. 'Look.'

Jean-Pierre followed her horrified gaze. They watched as the mangled paw at their feet began to change. The hairs were shrivelling away, revealing smooth, white flesh. The claws were stretching out to become fingers, human fingers, long, waxen and tapering. On one of the fingers was a ring with a sparkling amber stone. It was Gaston's ring.

'It was him!' whispered Jean-Pierre. 'All the time, it was him. We never knew . . .'

Marie shuddered. 'I saw his eyes as it came for me. I knew then . . .' She was crying. 'He said it was you. He tried to make everyone think that you were the werewolf, and all along it was him.'

CHAPTER XV

Thaт nigнт тне horrified magistrate took in the two young people.
They were exhausted and bleed-
ing, hardly aware until then that the wolf's
claws had injured them both. The doctor
was called. He and the magistrate listened
grimly as Jean-Pierre and Marie told their
tale. They examined the grisly relic that
lay in Marie's basket.

That same night the magistrate took six
of the town guard and rode to the
château. They broke down the great oak
door. They discovered Gaston lying on the
floor of his chamber under the wolfskins.
Bloody rags were wrapped around the
stump of his severed arm.

They searched the château. From the cellars they took away all the evidence of
Gaston's hideous experiments. Gaston's
trial lasted for many months. Among the
witnesses called was the young lawyer

who had chanced upon that terrible scene on the forest road five years before, and the coachman himself was finally tracked down. He revealed everything. The deaths of the Count and Countess de Guise and Marie's father were counted among the victims of Gaston's terrible crimes.

Gaston de Guise was sentenced to be burnt at the stake and with him all the terrible instruments of his secret art, all the barbarous contents of that cellar. All manuscripts and documents were to be destroyed with him. Nothing was to remain. The flames burnt for three days and nights.

For Jean-Pierre and Marie the long nightmare was at last over. That summer they were married and became the next Count and Countess de Guise. There was great joy and celebration in the village. The estate was restored to its former splendour. The château of Guise became famous all around for the extraordinary beauty of its gardens. The roses bloomed once more, the doves returned to the dovecot and the villagers slept peacefully in their beds. Each winter the wolves returned to the valley, but after the fearful, solitary howl of the werewolf, their mournful chorus was almost welcome.

Blood Dance
by LOUISE COOPER

CHAPTER I

IN HER DREAM Garland was two years old again, and very frightened.

Somehow, she knew she was dreaming. But in a way that only made matters worse, for the strangeness of being very small gave the nightmare an even more chilling edge. And something about it was frighteningly, horribly *real*. Almost as if it had all happened before . . .

In the dream it was night. Garland had woken suddenly, to hear a strange sound outside in the darkness of the forest beyond her house. She had begun to cry, and almost at once her mother came hurrying in. But though she hugged Garland and soothed her, Garland knew something was wrong. And now, by the unsteady light of one candle that cast menacing shadows on the ceiling, Garland huddled, trembling, in her mother's arms, listening as the sound out there in the night grew louder and closer. She had never heard such a sound before and hoped with all her heart that she would never have to hear it again. A rhythmic *thud ... thud ... thud* as something she couldn't name and couldn't imagine moved slowly, grimly past the house along the forest track. It sounded almost like men marching. But Garland knew in her bones that it was not. Whatever stirred out there in the night was something far stranger, and as she turned her head fearfully towards the curtained window of her bedroom she heard her mother's voice say softly and quickly:

'There's no need to be afraid, little one. They won't hurt us. But we must not look out of the window tonight. Whatever we do, we must not look outside!'

Thud ... thud ... thud ... The sounds continued, each one driving a new arrow of terror into Garland's heart. The candle flame wavered, and the shadows on the ceiling seemed to quake in time with the awful, steady marching rhythm. Then suddenly the candle-light flared, brightened, seemed to fill the room –

And she woke to the first, pale light of a summer dawn.

Garland sat up in bed, shivering as the last tatters of the dream fled from her mind. *That nightmare again.* She *had* had it before. In fact it had haunted her for thirteen years, and every time it was exactly the same. The dim room, the eerie sounds, her mother's words of warning . . . it had all seemed so real. And, as she had done many times before, Garland asked herself if perhaps it was. Had the events of her dream actually happened to her when she was very small? She would have been too young to remember such a thing clearly. But was she reliving an episode from her own past?

She could have asked her mother, of course. But somehow she had never quite plucked up the courage. Once, a year or so ago, she had tried to drop hints about the dream, hoping that her questions might be answered. But her mother had brushed her hesitant words aside, saying quickly that dreams were harmless and meaningless and Garland shouldn't worry herself over nothing. She had then firmly changed the subject. As if, or so it seemed to Garland, she wanted to pretend that the matter had never been raised.

Garland frowned at that thought, then abruptly pushed it away. Her room was shadowy; she wanted suddenly to banish the shadows, for they reminded her too much of the dream. So, slipping out of bed, she ran to her window to pull back the curtains and look out at the day. The forest was dense and the trees encroached almost to their garden wall. But this morning even their dark gloominess couldn't bring a chilly little tingle to her skin as it usually did. For above the trees the sky was starting to turn from the watery gold of sunrise to a bright, clear blue. There wasn't a cloud to be seen; the world looked bright and fresh, and as she looked at the scene the last of Garland's unease faded away and she smiled. She wasn't going to let any nightmare spoil her joy this morning. For today was a great milestone in her life. More than that; it was the *happiest* day of her life. For this was the day when she would officially become betrothed to Coryn.

Her thoughts seemed to take wing then, and fly to the grander, older house, three miles away on the far side of the forest, where Coryn lived with his widowed mother. Garland and Coryn had known each other since they were children, and from the very beginning Garland had fallen in love with the tall, blond-haired boy with his quiet blue eyes and gentle smile. Coryn wasn't like the other boys of the farms and villages in the district. Where they enjoyed fighting and horseplay, he loved music and books. And dancing. That, Garland reflected, was what had truly brought them together, for dancing was one of her own greatest pleasures. Then, when she was thirteen and Coryn fifteen, they had partnered each other at the Harvest Fair and her secret dream had come true. For, when the first dance ended, Coryn had held on to her hands and, gazing into her eyes, had told her that he loved her.

Garland would remember for ever just how he had looked in that memorable moment. So solemn, so serious – and so afraid that she might scorn him, or even laugh at him. And she remembered, too, how his look of uncertainty had changed to a look of joy as she shyly told him that there could never be anyone else for her.

Two years had passed since that momentous evening. In that time, their love had grown stronger – and now a final crown was about to be set on Garland's happiness. Her parents and Coryn's mother had agreed to a match between their children. And tonight, at Coryn's house, a great party would take place to celebrate their betrothal.

They wouldn't marry for several years, of course, for they were both too young. But Garland was content to wait. She would wear a silver ring on her finger, Coryn's betrothal gift, and the world would know that they belonged to each other. And when a few years had passed and they *were* married, then a whole new life would begin for them both. They would be so happy. They would –

'Garland!' Her mother's voice called suddenly from downstairs. 'Garland, are you awake?'

Garland snapped out of her daydream. 'Yes, Mother!' she called back.

'Then hurry and dress yourself, child. Breakfast will be early today; there's a great deal to do.'

The gown she would wear tonight was laid on a chair. Blue brocade – the blue of Coryn's eyes – and stitched with pearls that were starting to shine as the sunlight through her window grew stronger. Garland felt a joyous urge to try it on just one more time, but quelled the impulse. Only a few more hours, and evening would come. She had waited two years for this. She could contain her impatience for a little while longer . . .